# You Want It?
# Just Ask
# Complete Series

# You Want It?
# Just Ask
# Complete Series

BY

TRACY WILSON

Published by
Beautiful Publications LLC
Stratford, CT 06614

This book is a work of fiction. Names, characters, places, and incidents are either products of the author's imagination or are used fictitiously. Any resemblance to actual events or locales or persons, living or dead, is entirely coincidental.

©Copyright 2023 Tracy Wilson

Library of Congress Control Number:
2023900838
PRINT ISBN:   979-8-9871005-9-2
EBOOK ISBN: 979-8-9871005-6-1
EBOOK ISBN: 979-8-9871005-7-8
EBOOK ISBN: 979-8-9871005-8-5


Printed in the United States of America

You Want It? Just Ask

# You Want It? Just Ask

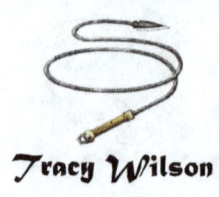

When we got there, two body guards were standing outside. There were about 100 people in front of us but the line moved quickly. When we finally got up to the entrance they took our coats, checked them for us, and escorted us to the 'Blue Room.' The walls were sky blue, there was plush navy blue carpeting on the floor, and there were two navy blue leather sectionals on the wall directly in front of us, two navy blue leather sectionals on the left, and two navy blue leather sectionals on the right. In front of each sectional was an aquarium glass table so you could see the fish as you sat and ate and drank. There was a small bar and jazz was playing as the room filled up with people sitting, chatting, drinking, dancing, and ordering at the bar.

As Jordan and I were sipping on some champagne, the 1st body guard came into the room and announced, "Make

yourselves comfortable – you'll be here for a while." Jordan and I continued to sip on our champagne as we watched the room empty out slowly.

When it was our turn, the 1st body guard came into the room again... "Jordan and Trenice follow me," he said mischievously as we followed him out of the 'Blue Room' and we were escorted down a winding corridor until we came upon another line of people. We could see they were the same people we came in with.

"I guess this is part of the process honey," I said.

"I guess so – if they're willing to go through all this, it must be worth it," Jordan said.

"Jake and Rachel come here so I know it's worth it. I wonder why they told us not to come on Tuesday night — it sure seems to be jumpin' in here," I said.

"Shit if Tuesday is their slow night; imagine what the weekends are like!" Jordan laughed.

"I don't think I wanna come in here on the weekend — be just our luck to run into someone we know," I laughed.

It was finally our turn as the two body guards showed up again. "Spread your arms out to the side and spread your legs please," the 1st body guard said.

"For what?" Jordan asked.

"Sir we need to search everyone that comes in here as a precaution — it's for your own protection." I was tired of

standing with my legs and arms apart so I brought them back together and folded my arms while I waited for Jordan to finish...

"Sir, please let us finish the search..."

"Why you gotta be all up my leg – damn!"

"Sorry sir – we need to check for concealed weapons and drugs – it'll just take a few minutes..." Jordan spread his legs again and sucked his teeth along with two guys behind him.

As he was being searched the lady standing behind me leaned forward and whispered in my ear, "Hmmm.... Nice ass...."

I jerked around quicker than Linda Blair in the Exorcist... "Excuse me?"

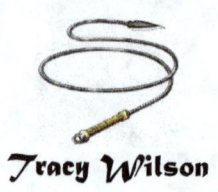

*Tracy Wilson*

"Oh... I said he has a nice ass... something wrong?"

Unbeknownst to me, Jordan was standing there grinning from ear to ear but I caught him out the side of my eye when I replied, "Oh no – nothing's wrong at all – in fact, I couldn't agree with you more..."

"Madam spread your legs please

"Damn Trenice – I knew this shit would happen..." Jordan sighed.

"Oh I get it – Nancy can you check her please?"

"Why can't you?" I asked.

"Company policy forbids me from checking bare asses Madam – step over

## You Want It? Just Ask

here please..." Jordan glared at me until I flashed him a mischievous grin, placed my finger in my mouth, and licked it seductively while Nancy made sure I didn't have anything concealed.

"I thought so..." my new friend whispered in my ear as she playfully slapped my bare ass. Before she could pull her hand away I grabbed it, twisted it, and pulled her directly in front of me.

"Next time ask before you touch," I said as I pulled her face to mine and forced my tongue in her mouth. The crowd behind us roared with approval.

"Woo hoo!"

"I can't wait to play with them!"

"We got us a couple a newbie freaks!"

"Damn!"

As we went through the metal detectors we were escorted down another corridor to the 'Red Room.' The 'Red Room' had bright red walls and deep red plush carpeting and everyone was standing, including the members that followed us into the room along with the body guards. The 1st body guard made the following announcement:

"Attention Newbies! Before you step inside I will go over the rules. After each rule you must raise your right hand and repeat that you understand and accept the rule. Here are the rules."

"**Rule #1.** We have received your applications for membership. Our committee has reviewed your applications and you have all been invited here tonight based on your answers to our questions in

the application. Once it is determined that you have met the qualifications for membership, my partner will nominate you all for membership – however, your nominations must be 2$^{nd}$ by a member of 'Just Ask.' Once that is done my partner will ask if it is unanimous. If all members here tonight agree, then – and only then – will you become members of 'Just Ask.' If you understand and accept this rule, raise your right hands and repeat, we understand and accept this rule."

We all raised our right hands and repeated in unison, "We understand and accept this rule."

"**Rule #2**. Everything is consensual. At no time is anyone to force anything on anybody. No means no. If you violate this rule not only will you be barred from this establishment but you will also be escorted out of here in handcuffs and

charged with rape.  If you understand and accept this rule, raise your right hands and repeat, we understand and accept this rule."

"We understand and accept this rule."

"**Rule #3**.  The only video cameras allowed in this establishment are the video cameras we provide.  If you violate this rule not will you be barred from this establishment but your camera will be confiscated, you will also be escorted out of here in handcuffs,  and you will be charged with violating the member's right to privacy.  If you understand and accept this rule, raise your right hands and repeat, we understand and accept this rule."

"We understand and accept this rule."

## You Want It? Just Ask

"**Rule #4.** All activities are monitored in this establishment. You are under constant surveillance. If you understand and accept this rule, raise your right hands and repeat, we understand and accept this rule."

"We understand and accept this rule."

"**Rule #5.** Clothing is optional. You must wear clothing to enter this establishment but once you go through those doors you may remove your clothing if you wish; however, if you chose not to remove your clothing that is your prerogative. If you understand and accept this rule, raise your right hands and repeat, we understand and accept this rule."

"We understand and accept this rule."

"**Rule #6**. If you engage in sexual activities with multiple partners you must use condoms! If you violate this rule not only will you be barred from this establishment but you will also be escorted out of here in handcuffs and you will not be released until you have submitted to a blood test for STD's and we will notify our members if those results are positive so they will know they have been put at risk. If you understand and accept this rule, raise your right hands and repeat, we understand and accept this rule."

"We understand and accept this rule."

"**Rule #7**. If you wish to record any sexual activities between you and other

## You Want It? Just Ask

partners you must request this along with all other participants. Each participant must sign an affidavit consenting to be videotaped and a camera will be provided for you; however, you will not be able to copy the tape unless you bring it to us and all participants sign an affidavit giving us permission to copy the tape. If you try to copy the tape on your own you will end up with a distorted picture. If you understand and accept this rule, raise your right hands and repeat, we understand and accept this rule."

"We understand and accept this rule."

"**Rule #8**. You may only use toys provided by this establishment. If you try to conceal any toys and bring them in they will be confiscated and will not be returned to you. All toys must be purchased here for everyone's protection.

If you understand and accept this rule, raise your right hands and repeat, we understand and accept this rule."

"We understand and accept this rule."

"**Rule #9**. What goes on here stays here. If you violate this rule you will be barred from this establishment. If you understand and accept this rule, raise your right hands and repeat, we understand and accept this rule."

"We understand and accept this rule."

"**Rule #10**. If you get drunk or if we feel you are incapable of driving we are taking your keys – period! You can pick up your car within the next 24 hours. If you understand and accept this rule, raise your right hands and repeat, we understand and accept this rule."

"We understand and accept this rule."

"**Rule #11**. Cell phones, pagers, etc. are prohibited in this establishment. If we find any cell phones, pagers, etc., we will ask you to step off the line, go put your cell phones, pagers, etc. in your car, or go home. Besides the fact that you can barely hear one another, our members don't come here to talk on the phone – they come here to relax, relate, and release – no holds barred! This also protects our members from being photographed without their consent and, more importantly, this also protects you from being escorted out of here in handcuffs and being charged with violating the member's right to privacy. If you understand and accept this rule, raise your right hands and repeat, we understand and accept this rule."

"We understand and accept this rule."

"**Rule #12**. Leave your problems outside. No one came here to hear about your problems. Everyone comes here to relax, relate, and release — no holds barred! If you understand and accept this rule, raise your right hands and repeat, we understand and accept this rule."

"We understand and accept this rule."

"Very good — I.D.'s please?" After all our I.D.'s were checked we were all given our membership cards. "You have all met the requirements for membership and you have all stated that you understood and accepted our rules. I nominate you all as our newest members of Just Ask!"

## You Want It? Just Ask

"I 2nd the nomination!" my new best friend yelled out.

"So say you all?" the 2nd body guard asked.

"So say we all!" they yelled in unison.

"You have been nominated and accepted by all!  Welcome to Just Ask! Enjoy your stay!" the 2nd body guard yelled as the double doors opened, streamers and balloons came out of the ceiling, and we were all presented with a glass of champagne while being escorted through the double doors.  My new best friend was right on my heels along with her husband as we went through the doors.

I started praying immediately... "Lord please don't let us wind up in jail," I prayed as her husband grabbed Jordan

*Tracy Wilson*

around the waist and started kissing him on the back of the neck...

# You Want It? Just Ask

Tracy Wilson

# You Want It?
# Just Ask 2

## You Want It? Just Ask

"Oh hell no!" Jordan yelled as he turned around and was face to face with her husband.

"Something wrong?" he asked.

"You gotta back up off me with that," Jordan said as he pushed her husband away from him.

As her husband put his hands up and backed away from Jordan his wife pulled me close to her and started kissing me on my neck as she said, "I thought we could play with you..."

"We wanna play – but not with you," I snapped as I pushed her back.

"Ouch!" she said hastily.

"Awww... c'mere sweetie," I said as I took her hand. "I'm sorry - I didn't mean

to hurt your feelings. It's just that were not bi-sexual."

"Oh...well why didn't you say so?" she said as she went over to Jordan and grabbed his ass while her husband palmed mine.

When she reached down to grab his cock Jordan grabbed her hand... "Stop it!" he laughed.

"Don't you like me?" she pouted as she laid her head in Jordan's chest...

"I like you a lot – but I love her," he said as he pulled me away from her husband.

"Oh...I see," she laughed as she went back to her husband. "Mind if we show you around?" she asked as she playfully wrapped her arm around Jordan's waist.

## You Want It? Just Ask

"Sure why not?" I said as I wrapped my arm around her husband's waist and we all proceeded down the corridor.

"I'm Susan and this is my husband, John."

"Oh no!" I said mockingly as if I were shocked.

"What's wrong?" she asked.

"You kissed and told!" I laughed.

"Ha ha ha – very funny Trenice," she said as we all laughed. There was a dance party going on below us on the lower level as we continued to walk down the corridor and we stopped in front of the toy store.

"Woo hoo – toys!" I yelled.

*Tracy Wilson*

"You like to play with toys?" Susan asked seductively.

"I love to play – period."

"Damn right!" Jordan yelled.

"A man after my own heart – I mean Trenice's heart," John laughed.

"Damn right!" Jordan yelled again as we all laughed and walked into the store.

"So you like movies?" Susan asked.

"Making them or watching them?" I asked.

"Both."

"I like 'em both," I said.  John and Jordan looked at us then at each other.  I

think we all knew where this night was gonna end up.

"I love their dildo collection honey – look – this cock's taller than me!" I laughed as I ran up to it and stood beside it.

"Ohh...I'd love to ride that," Susan said as she came and stood beside me.

"Your ass would get stuck too," John hollered.

"Not necessarily," I said matter-of-factly. The look Jordan, John, and Susan gave me was priceless.

"How the hell can you ride that and not get stuck?" John asked. Jordan grinned and shook his head.

"Yo man – she for real?" John asked.

"Let her tell you," Jordan laughed.

"Please tell me," Susan begged.

"Ok, ok, ok.  You know what a **'Chin-Up'** is right?"

"Um….yea."

"Well I'm about to tell you what the **'Low Down'** is."

"Ok."

"You put a pole in the doorway of your bedroom, making sure you leave enough space for your head – just like when you do a chin-up."  As I turned to the right I saw I had an audience.

"Then what Trenice?"

## You Want It? Just Ask

"After you grab the pole, have your husband measure the distance from your pussy to the floor so you know how many inches in height the standing dildo should be. Then, measure your husband's cock or your favorite dildo and add that to the distance from your pussy to the floor. For example: if you take a 9 inch cock and the distance from your pussy to the floor is 24 inches, you add 9 inches to that and get a standing dildo that's 33 inches in height. This way when you lower yourself onto it, it's the perfect fit and it stays put."

Jordan continued laughing as he saw some people taking notes.

"Damn Trenice – how you know that?"

"How you think I know that?" I hollered. Jordan and John were hunched over holding their stomachs laughing, the

sale associates were grinning from ear to ear, and the standing dildos started disappearing off the shelves.

As the line grew longer, Susan pulled me to the side and whispered in my ear, "So how did you know I take a 9 inch cock?"

"You grabbed one earlier," I whispered back as I pointed at Jordan.

"You ready Trenice?" Jordan asked as he came up behind me.

"Not yet honey – I wanna look at the rest of the toys," I said as I walked past the lingerie and headed straight for the leather outfits – chains with cuffs, whips, collars, leashes, blindfolds, paddles – you name it – they had it.

## *You Want It? Just Ask*

"You wanna spankin' baby?" Susan asked as John came up behind her, caressing her breasts.

"I've been a naughty boy and I need to be punished," he said as she leaned back into him while caressing his cock with her hand behind her back. "Punish me baby," he moaned as she continued to rub his cock.

"I see you like to watch," Susan said as Jordan and I looked on.

"Oh yea!" we said in unison.

"We like to watch too," she said seductively.

"Come with me," I said as I took her hand. Jordan knew where I was headed but John had no idea.

"Damn – I gotta give you your props Jordan," I heard John say as Susan and I walked ahead of them.

"Where are you taking me Trenice?"

"To bed," I said.

"Oohhhh…I like the sound of that," she said as we stopped when we got in the back corner of the toy store. "You sure seem to know your way around Trenice – you sure you haven't been here before?"

"No I haven't – but I know where to find my toys once you let me loose in the store," I laughed.

"So what are we doing here?" John asked.

"Watch," I said. John looked at Jordan while shrugging his shoulders.

## You Want It? Just Ask

"Sir, would you take down that bed please?" I asked.

"Sure thing Madam," the associate said as he placed the velvet inflatable mattress on the floor. We already had a few spectators but I knew more would come once we got started.

"Coming Honey?" I asked.

"Not yet, but I will be," Jordan said as he lay down on the mattress on his back.

"Oh yea!" John said as I placed Jordan's hands in the top restraints and cuffed his wrists.

"Susan would you like to…" Before I could finish my sentence, she placed

Jordan's feet in the bottom restraints and cuffed his feet.

"Oh baby are you gonna get it," she said to her husband as she got up. I got down on the floor, crawled on top of Jordan, slowly and deliberately, stopping to unzip his pants, and took his cock out.

"Woo hoo!"

"Yea baby!"

"Now that's what I'm talking about!"

"Ride that shit!" I heard from the crowd as I eased up my skirt and slid myself down on his cock. Susan and John started caressing each other as I rode Jordan's cock, moaning as he began pushing and thrusting up inside me.

## You Want It? Just Ask

"Can we come with you?" Susan breathed as John bent her over and thrust his cock in her from behind...

"Oh yesss – come with us..." I moaned as John squatted against the wall and Susan squatted in front of him, thrusting herself on John's cock while Jordan was thrusting his cock up inside me. To the right of me another couple was masturbating each other as we continued to writhe in the throes of ecstasy.

"Oh God it feels so good..." Susan moaned.

"That's it – ride my cock baby," Jordan said as he continued thrusting his cock up inside me.

"I'm cummin'...I'm cummin'..."

*Tracy Wilson*

"You cummin' baby? I'm cummin' with you..." Susan, John, and everyone else that joined in the orgy followed suit.

"Oh shit...I'm gonna cum too..."

"I'm cummin which y'all..."

"This is so hot...I wanna come on your ass baby..."

"Fuck me!"

"Harder!"

"Oh that's it – right there..."

"Oh shit..."

"Here I come..."

"Oh..."

## *You Want It? Just Ask*

"Agghhh…"

"Uhh huh…uhh huh…"

"Yes…Yes…Yes…"

"Don't stop…"

"Aggggghhhhh!!!"

I collapsed on top of Jordan, John collapsed on top of Susan as she fell down on top of us, and everyone applauded.

"We'll take one of these," Susan said nearly out of breath. Everyone else that joined in the orgy followed suit.

"Yea we want one too!"

"My man! Over here!"

"Me too man!"

John and Susan got up off of us and Susan helped me undo the restraints.

"That was fuckin' hot!" she yelled.

"Damn right!" Jordan yelled back.

"I'll meet you in front baby," John said as he came back with his bed-in-a-bag.

"Okay baby," Susan said as she put her hand between his legs and rubbed his cock while kissing him. "How you know about that Trenice?" she asked.

"How you think she knows about it?" Jordan laughed.

As we walked towards the exit to the main corridor Susan stopped in front of the swing. "Oh boy – I've always wanted

one of these!" Jordan and I bust out laughing. "This too? Damn!" she laughed. When we got into the corridor, Susan asked her husband, "Sweetie can you buy me a swing?"

"Only if you promise to punish me," he said seductively.

As we continued down the corridor there were 8 rooms on the left and 8 rooms on the right. Each room had a window with a curtain and if the curtain was left open, you were welcome to watch. The 1st room had 3 girls going at each other with their mouths and dildos. We watched as they took turns using the **'Anal Tickler Vibrator'** on each other. Each girl would put it on her finger then tickle another girl's ass while eating her pussy.

"Wanna join them?" Susan asked.

"Naaa..." I said as we continued down the corridor.

The 2nd room had 4 guys taking turns – first they all laid down and sucked each other's cocks in a circle then they took turns doing each other from behind. When we got to the 3rd room I started pulling on Jordan really hard...

"Wait a minute Trenice – I'm looking at what's going on over here..."

"Look Jordan – look!" I yelled as I yanked him over to the window.

"Damn! So that's why they told us not to come on Tuesday nights!" Jordan yelled.

"Friends of yours?" John asked.

"Yea," I said.

## You Want It? Just Ask

"I know how you feel – we came in here and caught my parent's goin' at it once," Susan said.

"Eww!" we said in unison.

"You think your parents stopped fuckin' Trenice?" Susan asked.

"Oh please – my grandparents are still fuckin' – my grandmother saw one of my nighties and told me it was too revealing."

"Really?" Susan asked.

"Yea. She should'a stopped there though," I said.

"Why Trenice?"

"She proceeded to tell me my grandfather prefers everything to be covered up so he can feel his way around," I laughed.

"Oh my God – some people get blue eyes from their parents – you got freakiness from yours!" Susan laughed. Everyone else bust out laughing along with us. "There are 5 more rooms on this side – lets finish viewing the rooms on this side, then we'll go up to the other side," Susan said.

"Sounds good Susan," Jordan said as he put his arm around Susan's waist and John put his arm around mine. We continued to stand there and look in the window as Jake had '**4 For 1**' – he was on his back while Rachel sat on his face, another woman was riding his cock, and he had a pussy to play with in each hand. We continued to watch everyone writhing

### You Want It? Just Ask

in ecstasy and then it was Rachel's turn for '5 For 1' – one man laid down on the bed and Rachel sat backwards on his cock, sliding it into her ass, then she leaned back on him taking another cock in her mouth as Jake climbed on top of her and slid his cock in her pussy, then two more men joined in and she jerked their cocks – one in each hand. We watched until they all exploded in ecstasy – there was so much squirting going on, sperm was hitting the window.

"Woo hoo!"

"Yea Baby!"

"That was fuckin' hot!"

"I thought I'd seen it all!"

"Damn that shit has me so wet!"

"Hard cock here – any takers?"

"Bring it on baby!"

"Were you at?"

"Over here baby," another woman yelled as she propped herself up on the wall, legs spread wide. The man she was waiting for came up to her, dropped to his knees, and started eating her pussy right then and there.

"Woo hoo!"

"Tear that pussy up!"

"Suck that clit!"

"Le'me have soma dat!" another man yelled as the 1st man moved out the way so the 2nd man could indulge.

## You Want It? Just Ask

"You ready for this hard cock baby?" the 1st man said as he was stroking himself.

"Yes baby – give it to me – please give it to me..." she gasped as he thrust his cock up inside her while we all looked on. We walked down the corridor to the 4th room and watched a couple playing in the swing.

"I hope the beams are sturdy," Jordan said as she switched positions with her husband.

"We haven't seen anyone break a leg yet," John said.

"I bet Trenice has – huh Trenice?" Susan asked.

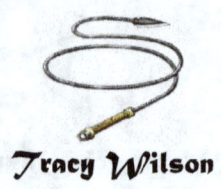

"I haven't actually seen anyone break a leg – but I sure know what it feels like," I laughed.

"Damn! Is there anything you two haven't done?" Susan asked.

"Ask me that question again after tonight," I laughed.

"Where the hell have you two been all my life?" Susan laughed.

We walked down to the 5$^{th}$ room and saw another couple paying with switches, chains, etc.

"Oh I'm gonna spank that ass real good tonight baby," Susan said.

"Promises, promises," John laughed.

## You Want It? Just Ask

We walked down to the 6th room and watched a couple giving each other **'Icy Body Parts'** – they took turns melting ice cubes on each other while sucking each other's nipples, belly's, thighs, and legs.

"That looks like a fun way to cool off," I laughed.

"Oh it is; it is!" John laughed.

The grand finale was when he picked up the bottle of champagne out of the bucket, took some of the crushed ice, and packed her pussy with it. "Woo hoo! I know that shit is cold!" I yelled.

"More like frozen!" Susan laughed. We continued to watch as he open the bottle of champagne, poured the champagne into her pussy, and had **'Champagne on Ice'** as he sucked the champagne out of her pussy.

"Damn!" Jordan and John yelled in unison.

"Anybody thirsty?" I asked seductively.

"Oh yea baby I'm real thirsty!" someone yelled behind us.

"Me too – leave some for us my man!" another man yelled in back of us.

We walked down to the 7th room and watched another couple give each other '**A Little Pain, A Lot of Pleasure**' as she picked up one of the candles, straddled her man, and slowly dripped hot wax from his chest down to his belly, kissing each spot on the way down. When she got to his cock she put the candle down and put his cock in her mouth, took it out to lick it,

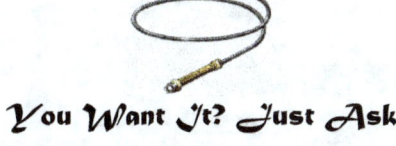

kiss the shaft, jerk it, and then put it back in her mouth again.

"I was waiting to see if she was gonna drip hot wax on his cock," I laughed.

"Me too Trenice," Susan said.

"Ain't no way in hell," Jordan said.

"You should try it sometime," John said.

"Naa... Trenice's mouth is hot enough – I don't need burning wax on top a dat," Jordan laughed. We continued to watch as she got on her hands and knees and he dripped candle wax on her back down to her ass as he fucked her from behind. When we got to the 8th room, we watched another couple start out in the missionary position, then he got up and

proceeded to give her a **'Black Kiss'** – he started out by sucking her clit, then he tongued her pussy, then he tongued her ass.

"Eww!" Susan and I said in unison.

"What's wrong with that?" John asked.

"He's gonna kiss her after that!" I yelled.

"Yea? So?"

"So she's gonna taste her own shit!" I yelled. Everyone behind me bust out laughing.

"You really think they don't clean their ass before they do that Trenice?" John laughed.

## You Want It? Just Ask

"It's just the idea of it - I wouldn't wanna kiss you after you ate my ass," I laughed.

"I have to agree with Trenice honey," Susan said.

"Oh yea? You didn't say that the other night," John laughed. Everyone behind us bust out laughing again as the man got on his back and received a **'Black Kiss'** from his woman. We turned around to start on the next row of rooms. The 1st room had two couples. Each couple was wearing leather outfits that covered their body from head to toe. We watched as they rubbed up against one another, exploring each other's bodies as the men stopped to caress the woman's breasts and palm their asses, while the women rubbed the men's cocks through their outfits until they were bulging. We walked down to the 2nd room and watched another couple

as they played with **'Latex Body Paint.'** The man poured the latex paint onto the woman's body and then waited for it to harden. Once the latex was hard on her body, she came up to the window while we were watching her and pressed her breasts up against the window so we could see how the latex hugged her curves. We continued to watch as he tore a piece of the latex off her nipple with his teeth, then he slowly and deliberately pulled latex off her breast as he sucked her nipple, then he began kissing her breast as he pulled more latex off her body from her neck, down her back, uncovering her ass.

"Now that looks interesting," I said.

"Oh my God – I don't believe it!"

"What Susan?"

## You Want It? Just Ask

"There actually is something you haven't done yet," she said as we all laughed.

When we got to the 3$^{rd}$ room it was set up like a work space – there was a table with tools on it and a work bench.

"How do you get into one of these rooms?" I asked.

"Oh that's easy," Susan said. "If a room is open, you go in, and do what you wanna do. If you wanna reserve a room in advance, you let management know about a month in advance. If you see something you like and you wanna join in, you can do that too as long as you're invited in."

"Sounds good," Jordan said as we watched the man undo his overalls and let them drop to the floor. We continued to watch as he took the woman by the hand,

led her to the work bench and asked her to **'Bend Over Baby'** as he bent her over the work bench, tied her hands and feet to the bottom of the legs to the bench, lifted up her skirt, and slid his cock up inside her while spanking her ass.

"Hey baby – don't we have a workbench in the garage?" John asked.

"As a matter-of fact we do," Susan laughed.

"What happens if you can't get in a room because they're always booked?" I asked.

"Most people just do what they wanna do wherever they find a spot – like some of the couples did tonight. See that couple down there?" Susan asked as she pointed to a couple on the dance floor.

## You Want It? Just Ask

"Yea."

"Some people just do that and don't bother coming up to this level. Some people just come here just to get their dance on and their drink on and then they go home."

"I don't think I'd ever do that."

"You don't drink Trenice?"

"Oh yea – I mean have sex with Jordan on the dance floor."

"Why not?" John asked.

"I dunno – it just doesn't do anything for me – I may get worked up on the dance floor but I think I'd wanna work out up here."

"I agree," Jordan said.

*Tracy Wilson*

When we got to the 4th room it was actually set up as a bathroom with a tub and shower. We watched as the couple kissed, sucked, and caressed their soapy bodies underneath the shower.

"Now that's nice," I said.

"Looks kinda boring," John said.

"You and Susan don't take showers together?" Jordan asked.

"Sure we do – but we use soap shaped like dildos and we do it in different positions," John said.

"Remember when we broke the soap holder honey?" Susan laughed.

"Yea – I kinda got carried away when I put my leg up on it," he laughed.

"Sounds like y'all had a good time," Jordan said.

"Exactly – these two ain't doin' shit," John laughed as the woman put her **'Leg Up'** on his shoulder and he slid his cock up into her and started fucking her while standing straight up.

"I bet Susan can get her **'Leg Up'** like that," I said.

"As a matter of fact, she can," John laughed.

"Now that's what I'm talkin' about," Jordan said as the man stood up on the tub, grabbed the shower pole, extended his leg towards the sink, and proceeded to **'Lay Up'** as the woman started sucking his cock.

"That looks like fun – hope he doesn't slip," Susan laughed.

When we got to the 5th room we watched as the man tied the woman's feet together, turned her over and tied her hands behind her back, extended the rope from her hands to her feet, placed the rope in a knot, placed her onto a hook, and then hoisted her up into the air so she was **'Hung From The Ceiling,'** giving him easy access to her breasts, pussy, and ass.

"I don't know if I could do that," I said.

"I think you could," Susan said.

"I dunno – I'd be afraid the harness wouldn't hold me or the rope would break and I'd hit the floor," I laughed.

## You Want It? Just Ask

"I think we'll stick to swings," Jordan laughed.

When we got to the 6th room we watched as the man was on top of his woman and they were both writhing in ecstasy. When he collapsed on top of her we thought they were finished.

"Looks like we came too late," Jordan laughed.

"Look honey," Susan said as the woman took a 9 inch dildo out of the freezer and put it on. We continued to watch as the man got on his knees, sucked the cock for a few minutes, turned around, bent over, and spread his ass cheeks as the woman proceeded to 'Cold Cock' him.

"Oh hell no!" Jordan and John yelled in unison.

"Next!" Susan and I yelled in unison as the man strapped on the dildo and **'Cold Cocked'** her ass as he fucked her pussy.

When we got to the 7th room we watched as the couple dripped chocolate syrup on each other, picked up tubes of honey and squirted it all over each other, picked up cans of whipped cream and took turns hitting each other in the face and hair, then they hit each other with cherries, crumbed nuts, chopped fruit, and sprayed each other with more whipped cream. You could see them laughing as they fell on top of each other and began licking each other from head to toe, as the mat below them was covered in a mixture of everything they were licking off each other.

"Now that's what I'm talking about," Jordan said.

## You Want It? Just Ask

"That doesn't do anything for me," John said.

"Don't knock it 'till you've tried it my man," Jordan said.

"You two have actually done that?" Susan asked.

"Oh yea – nothing like having fun while you eat," I laughed.

"Kinda reminds me of a baby making a mess," Susan said.

When we got to the 8$^{th}$ room it was empty but there were some camcorders set up on tripods. "I wanna go in there!" I yelled as I grabbed Jordan, pushed him in the room, closed the door, and pulled the curtain closed.

*Tracy Wilson*

"Damn Trenice – you gonna leave them out there like that?"

"Naaa...," I said as I opened the door...

# You Want It? Just Ask

Tracy Wilson

# You Want It? Just Ask 3

## You Want It? Just Ask

"We were wondering how long you were gonna leave us out here," John laughed.

"Shut up," I said.

"Excuse me?" they both said in unison.

"You heard me."

"But Trenice..."

"I said shut up!"

"Yes Madam," Susan said.

"From this moment on you will address me as Mistress – do you understand?"

"Yes Mistress," they both said in unison.

"Very good.  Susan, open the curtain."  Susan did as she was told.

"Jordan, pick up the camcorder and start recording.

"Yes Madam – I mean yes Mistress," he laughed as he picked up the camcorder and started recording.

"The safe word is ENOUGH.  Use this word when you want to stop – is that understood?"

"Yes Mistress," they both said in unison.

"Very good."  I grabbed John by the waist of his pants and pushed him down on the bed.  "You've been a very bad boy haven't you John?"

## You Want It? Just Ask

"Yes Mistress."

"You know what happens when you've been bad don't you?"

"Yes Mistress…I get punished."

"Very good.  Susan get over here and take off his pants."

"Yes Mistress."  John proceeded to help her and I smacked his hand.

"Don't you move until I tell you to move!"

"Yes Mistress."

"Now turn your ass over."

"Yes Mistress."

"Susan come stand in front of me."

"Yes Mistress." She stood in front of me as I unbuttoned her blouse, removed it, and then proceeded to unhook her bra.

"Let me help you," she said.

"Did I ask you to help me?"

"No Mistress."

"Okay then," I said as I removed her bra. I proceeded to remove her skirt and then her panties. "John's been a bad boy Susan – he needs a spanking."

"Yes Mistress," she said as she started to spank her husband.

When she started gettin' a little carried away I yelled at her, "Stop it! He wasn't that bad," I laughed.

## You Want It? Just Ask

"He likes it," she said.

"What did I tell you?"

"I'm sorry Mistress – I'll stop."

"Very good. John, stick your ass up in the air."

"Yes Mistress."

"Susan, lay down on your back but hang your legs off the end of the bed down to the floor."

"Yes Mistress."

"John, put your cock in Susan's mouth so she can suck it."

"Yes Mistress." Jordan kept recording as Susan pulled John deeper into her mouth, grabbing his ass.

"Would you like another woman to join you?"

"Yes Mistress…Yes," they both said in unison. I invited another woman into the room to give them the pleasure of '**2 for 1.**'

"Get down there and eat her pussy while she sucks her husband's cock."

"Yes Mistress," the woman said and proceeded to do as she was told.

"John, get on your back."

"Yes Mistress."

"Take off your clothes," I told the other woman.

"Yes Mistress."

## You Want It? Just Ask

"Susan, sit on your husband's cock."

"Yes Mistress."

"Sit on his face so he can eat your pussy while he fucks his wife," I told the other woman.

"Yes Mistress." Jordan kept recording and I watched as they enjoyed themselves.

"Ok John, get up on your knees."

"Yes Mistress."

"Get on all fours and suck his cock," I told the other woman.

"Yes Mistress," she said as she did as she was told.

Tracy Wilson

"Susan you eat her pussy while she sucks John's cock."

"Yes Mistress."

"Okay – both of you lay on your back."

"Yes Mistress," they both said in unison.

"John, take turns with them."

"Yes Mistress," he said as he thrust his cock into his wife, then the other woman.

"Would you like someone else to join you?"

"Yes Mistress," they all said in unison. I invited another man into the room.

## You Want It? Just Ask

"Take off your clothes," I told the other man.

"Yes Mistress."

"Get on the bed on your knees."

"Yes Mistress."

"Susan, suck his cock while John fucks you from behind."

"Oh yes Mistress..." she said as they enjoyed themselves.

"Okay – now you suck John's cock while he fucks you from behind," I said to the other woman.

"Yes Mistress."

*Tracy Wilson*

"You and John get on your backs on the bed."

"Yes Mistress."

"You and Susan get on top of them and all of you do '**69**'!"

"Yes Mistress!" they all yelled in unison. People were banging on the glass as Jordan kept recording both couples doing '**69**' at the same time.

"Okay – everyone get up!"

"Yes Mistress," they all said in unison as they got up.

"You and Susan get on your backs."

"Yes Mistress."

"Okay boys – get to work and don't stop 'til you cum!"

## You Want It? Just Ask

"Yes Mistress!" they yelled in unison as they both climbed on top of them, thrusts their cocks inside them, and kept going until everyone was exploding in ecstasy. The crowd was banging on the window as the men collapsed on the women and they lay there in orgasmic afterglow.

"Well done students. Now get dressed."

"Yes Mistress," they all said in unison. After they got dressed, Jordan took the tape and we all walked out of the room into the corridor.

"Woo hoo!"

"Whistle!"

"Applause!"

*Tracy Wilson*

"Encore!"

"That was fuckin' hot!"

"Punish me next Mistress!"

"Spank my ass baby!"

"I'm kinda hungry," I said.

"Me too," Jordan said.

"Well we've definitely worked up an appetite – let's show 'em where the restaurant is baby," Susan said.

"Okay baby," John said. We went down to the dance floor level and 'Flashlight' was playing.

"Let's dance," I said as I grabbed Jordan onto the floor.

## You Want It? Just Ask

"Am I gonna get to eat tonight Trenice?" Jordan asked.

"Oh you'll eat - I promise," I laughed.

"Oooohhh... sounds kinky," Susan said as she and John followed us onto the dance floor.

When the song was finished we followed them to the restaurant and sat down. "Sure is dark in here," I said.

"The show's about to begin," Susan said.

"Oh – ok." The lights came up and there was a stage with 4 cages. In the 1st cage, a couple was going at it doggie style, in the 2nd cage, a woman was gettin' spanked with a whip, in the 3rd cage, two women were exploring each other's naked

bodies, and in the 4$^{th}$ cage, two men were doing the same thing.

"This goes on all the time?" Jordan asked.

"Yea man," John said.

"May I take your drink orders?" the waitress asked.

"Sure – we'll each have a long island iced tea," I said.

"Yes Mistress," Susan and John said in unison as we all bust out laughing.

"I didn't know you had it in you Trenice," Susan said.

"I didn't either. That was my 1$^{st}$ time."

## You Want It? Just Ask

"No shit!" John said.

"Yea man – we never did anything like that before," Jordan said.

"Well you sure seemed like you know what you were doing," Susan said.

"Oh I did – believe me," I laughed.

"Well I'm proud to have been your first," Susan laughed.

"They say your first time should be special and you both made it very special," I laughed.

"We enjoyed every minute of it," John said.

"Damn right!" Jordan hollered.

"Here are your drinks," the waitress said as she put them down. The glasses were shaped like dildos with a hole in the tip of the head where the straw was placed.

"Oohh... can I keep this glass?" I asked.

"Yes Madam. May I take your orders?"

"Yes – I'll have the pasta with chicken parmigiana."

"I'll have the same," Susan said.

"I'll have the pasta with sliced London broil," Jordan said.

"I'll have the same," John said.

## You Want It? Just Ask

"Would you like marinara sauce or alfredo?"

"I'll have marinara sauce," Susan said."

"I'll have alfredo," I said.

"We'll have that too," Jordan said.

"Sounds good," John said.

"Would you like soup or salad?"

"Salad," we all said in unison"

"I'll be back with your salads," the waitress said as we laughed.

"You two eat here often?" Jordan asked.

"We eat here all the time," John said.

"You'll love the food," Susan said.

"Look Jordan, she's spankin' him with the whip," I said as I pointed to the 1<sup>st</sup> cage.

"They do this throughout dinner?" Jordan asked.

"Yea," John said. The waitress dropped off our salads and we started to eat them.

"Look at the dessert menu Trenice," Susan said. Jordan and I both look on as I read the menu: "Bed Pan Sundae – your choice of toppings, Cocksicle (Vanilla/Chocolate), Boobsicle (Vanilla/Chocolate), Assorted Pastries (For Men), Assorted Pastries (For Women), Cakes, Pies, Etc."

## You Want It? Just Ask

"Wow," Jordan said.

"The pastries for men are shaped like women's body parts. The pastries for women are shaped like cocks," Susan said. "I guess those two would order pastries for men," Jordan said as he pointed to the cage with the two men in it.

"I guess so," John said. We finished our salads just as the food arrived. Susan and I got pasta shaped like little cocks and John and Jordan got pasta shaped like breasts.

"This is cute," I laughed.

"Yea – it is," Jordan laughed.

"May I take your order for dessert?" the waitress asked.

"I'll have the boobsicle, John said.

*Tracy Wilson*

"I'll have the assorted pastries for women," Susan said.

"We'll have the bed pan sundae," I said.

"Okay, what toppings would you like?"

"Put 'em all on – and make them both look like banana splits," Jordan said.

"I hope you like your dessert," John laughed.

"Why you say that man?"

"You'll see," Susan laughed.    We continued watching the show in the cages on stage as we finished eating.

## You Want It? Just Ask

When we finished our meals, the waitress came back over. "Shall I bring dessert?" she asked.

"Yes please," I said.

"Ok," she said as she walked away. When she came back to the table, she only had two desserts. "Your bed pan sundaes are coming now," she said as we looked at the cart approaching us.

"Oh hell no!" we yelled in unison. Susan and John bust out laughing.

"Something wrong?" the waitress asked.

"Hell yea – take that shit back – I ain't eatin' outta no damn bed pan!" I yelled.

"Damn right – take that shit outta here!" Jordan yelled.

"Very well then – but you'll have to pay for it sir," the waitress said.

"Bring it to another table – just get it outta here!" Jordan yelled.

"Okay sir," the waitress said as she walked away with the cart.

"Now that was funny," John laughed.
"You knew didn't you?" Jordan asked.

"Yea we knew," Susan laughed.

"You ever eat one of those?" I asked.

## You Want It? Just Ask

"Sure I have – I just tell them give me the sundae without the bed pan," she laughed.

"I can't get with that either man," John laughed.

"The idea of a bed pan is a complete turn off – I immediately see shit n piss," Jordan said.

"Exactly – some things don't belong at the dinner table," I said. We got up, paid the check, and went back upstairs.

"You ready to call it a night Trenice?" Susan asked.

"Yea – you ready honey?" I asked.

"Yea I'm ready alright," Jordan laughed.

"Well it was a pleasure meeting and fucking with both of you," Susan said as we gave each other a hug. When we got to the front door there were two packages for us.

"What's this?" Jordan asked.

"Compliments on the house," the 1st body guard said.

"Oh that's nice!" I said.

"We made a lot of money tonight after your instructions on the use of the standing dildo and your performances so management is giving you an assortment of toys from the store as well as four sets of glasses from the restaurant."

"Thank you!" I yelled.

## You Want It? Just Ask

"Um....are there any bed pans in there?" Jordan asked.

"Hell no!" the 1st body guard laughed.

"Good," Jordan said.

"Whew – you had me worried for a minute," he laughed.

"You'll both have to sign these affidavits before you leave," the 2nd body guard said.

"Oh yea – for the video – I forgot about that," I said.

"My man – you said we were under constant surveillance right?" Jordan asked.

"Yes sir."

"So you see everything that goes on in the rooms too?"

"Yes sir."

"So le'me ask you something…"

"Sir, no one sees the tapes unless they break the law and we have to present them for evidence. The tapes are reviewed every evening to make sure our members are complying with the rules. Ninety nine percent of the time the tapes are dated and placed in the vault."

"Oh – okay then," Jordan said.

"We had a great time," I said.

"Glad you enjoyed yourselves – please recommend this place to your

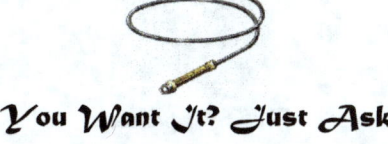

## You Want It? Just Ask

friends," the 1st body guard said as we left to go home.

Tracy Wilson